PAC
12/02

# Over the Candlestick

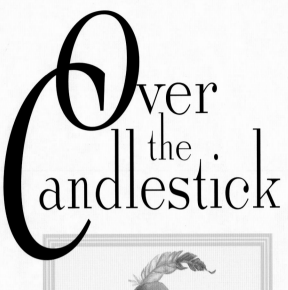

For my mom
—*M. G. M.*

Special thanks to
Franki Woodard,
Kay Johnson,
and Charles Slackman
for their helpful suggestions

Published by
PEACHTREE PUBLISHERS, LTD.
1700 Chattahoochee Avenue
Atlanta, Georgia 30318-2112

*www.peachtree-online.com*

Text © 2002 by Wayne Montgomery and Michael G. Montgomery
Illustrations © 2002 by Michael G. Montgomery

Manufactured in Singapore

Book design by Michael G. Montgomery and Loraine M. Balcsik
Text typeset in Goudy Infant by Fontographer and titles set in OPT Amadeus Solid
by Castcraft Software with initial capitals in Minion Swash Display by Adobe Systems
Full-color illustrations created in oil on canvas; spot drawings are in pencil on bond paper.

10 9 8 7 6 5 4 3 2 1
First Edition

**Library of Congress Cataloging-in-Publication Data**

Montgomery, Michael, 1952-
  Over the candlestick : classic nursery rhymes and the real stories behind them / written
and illustrated by Michael Montgomery.—
1st ed.
    p. cm.
Summary: Classic nursery rhymes are accompanied by historical background
information for the older reader.
  ISBN 1-56145-259-9
  1. Nursery rhymes. 2. Children's poetry. [1. Nursery rhymes.] I. Mother Goose.
English. II. Title.
  PZ8.3.M7812 Ov 2002
  398.8--dc21

2001005569

# Over the Candlestick

## Classic Nursery Rhymes

### AND THE

## REAL STORIES BEHIND THEM

COLLECTED BY WAYNE MONTGOMERY
AND MICHAEL G. MONTGOMERY
ILLUSTRATED BY MICHAEL G. MONTGOMERY

Ω
PEACHTREE
ATLANTA

# Table of Contents

Mary Had a Little Lamb ....................................................2

Little Miss Muffet.............................................................5

Jack Be Nimble .................................................................6

Hickory, Dickory, Dock....................................................7

London Bridge ..................................................................8

Old King Cole...................................................................11

Hush-a-bye, Baby .............................................................12

Ring-a-Ring o' Roses ........................................................13

Tom, Tom, the Piper's Son ..............................................14

Jack and Jill.......................................................................17

Humpty Dumpty...............................................................18

Hey Diddle Diddle ...........................................................20

Rain, Rain, Go Away.........................................................21

Yankee Doodle Dandy.......................................................23

Riddles...............................................................................24

Tongue Twisters.................................................................26

# *I*ntroduction

*M*ost of us are familiar with the charming rhymes, jingles, and limericks that we refer to collectively as nursery rhymes or Mother Goose songs. These simple compositions, which have endured for hundreds of years, are some of the best-known lines in the English-speaking world. While we may not remember exactly when we heard of Jack and Jill or who taught us the riddle of Humpty Dumpty, we have no trouble recalling the lyrics. And we can be reasonably certain that the lines we recite are very close to the original wording. We are certain because for generation after generation they have been repeated from parent to child to grandchild, largely unaltered. Some rhymes that appeared in print centuries ago have completely disappeared from written record, only to resurface in modern times. Amazingly, the oral renditions were almost identical to those in the first printed version.

Many of these familiar rhymes, however, so closely linked with earlier eras, raise questions in our times. Customs, kings, rituals, and practices celebrated in these rhymes no longer exist. Terms and phrases that were commonplace centuries ago now have little meaning for us. While much of a nursery rhyme's appeal lies in the musical rhythms and the repetitive phrases that are so satisfying to our ears, knowing a little about its origin and its connections to people and places long ago can certainly add to its charm. It can also add some entertainment value for the parent who's rapidly becoming tired of reading the same words aloud again and again. I never read these verses to my children without questions popping into my head. And it wasn't until I discovered THE ANNOTATED MOTHER GOOSE by the Baring-Goulds and THE OXFORD DICTIONARY OF NURSERY RHYMES that I found some of the answers.

It is not the intention of this book to analyze and dissect every line of each rhyme presented. It does not dwell upon the various possibilities concerning the morals or hidden meanings contained within them. It is merely a collection of some of the better-known rhymes presented in their earliest recorded form and a brief look at some of the real stories behind them.

I had always wondered why the idea of hanging a cradle in a treetop and its subsequent crash to the earth would be chosen to lull young children to sleep. I wanted to know the inside joke about a pony rider who put a feather in his cap and called it macaroni.

Now I know. And you can too.

— *Michael Montgomery*

# Mary Had a Little Lamb

Mary had a little lamb,
　　Its fleece was white as snow;
And everywhere that Mary went
　　The lamb was sure to go.

It followed her to school one day,
　　That was against the rule;
It made the children laugh and play
　　To see a lamb at school.

And so the teacher turned it out,
　　But still it lingered near,
And waited patiently about
　　Till Mary did appear.

Why does the lamb love Mary so?
　　The eager children cry;
Why, Mary loves the lamb you know,
　　The teacher did reply.

**"Mary had a little lamb" were the first words ever heard on Edison's phonograph.**

Written by Mrs. Sara Josepha Hale of Boston, this charming rhyme about a loyal lamb and its loving master contains four of the best-known lines in the English language. First published in 1830, the verse's popularity was immediate and widespread. A number of people came forth claiming to be the original Mary. The industrialist Henry Ford collected more than two hundred documents supporting one claimant and restored the old schoolhouse at Sudbury, Massachusetts, to commemorate the event. The author insisted that her work was not based on any particular incident; she also pointed out that many a pet lamb could have followed its owner to school. In 1877, Thomas Edison secured the rhyme's place in history when he chose "Mary had a little lamb" as the first sounds to be uttered by his new talking machine —the phonograph.

# Little Miss Muffet

Little Miss Muffet
Sat on a tuffet,
Eating her curds and whey;
There came a big spider,
Who sat down beside her
And frightened Miss Muffet away.

**The tuffet Miss Muffet sat on could have been a three-legged stool...**

**or a grassy hillock.**

Could the origin of "Little Miss Muffet" lie in the political intrigue of sixteenth century England? One scholar maintained that Mary, Queen of Scots, was Miss Muffet and the minister John Knox was the angry Presbyterian spider who wanted to frighten the Roman Catholic ruler away from the throne.

But more than likely, the skittish young subject of this popular rhyme was Patience Muffet, daughter of Dr. Thomas Muffet, a fifteenth-century entomologist. Dr. Muffet, particularly fond of spiders, composed a poem called "The Silkwormes and their Flies." It isn't too hard to imagine him writing for his daughter a ditty that features an unwelcome eight-legged guest.

Later versions of the rhyme substituted other young misses—"Little Mary Ester sat on a Tester," for example, or "Little Miss Mopsey sat on a Topsey"—but it was Miss Muffet who endured.

What exactly was a "tuffet?" A stool with a tufted cushion or a grassy knoll? In any case, it is harder to imagine why the spider would have wanted Miss Muffet's curds and whey—an appetizing blend of coagulated milk and watery cheese by-product.

# Jack Be Nimble

Jack be nimble,
Jack be quick,
Jack jump over
The candle stick.

Jack's desire for fame and fortune prompted him to leap the candlestick. While not exactly an Olympic event, candlestick jumping was once a popular game. Generations of Englishmen participated in the contests, knowing that the winner's prize was a year's supply of good luck. In some villages, candlestick jumping was the highlight of the festivities on St. Catherine's Day, November 25.

The rules were simple. A lighted candle was placed upon the floor. Those who could jump over the candle without putting out the flame were assured good fortune. Those who extinguished the flame (or caught fire) were not.

# Hickory, Dickory, Dock

Hickory, dickory, dock,
The mouse ran up the clock.
The clock struck one,
The mouse ran down,
Hickory, dickory, dock.

Hickory, Dickory, Dock" first appeared in print in TOM THUMB'S PRETTY SONG BOOK in 1744. Some believe that this rhyme originated with the shepherds in northwestern England, who used their own counting words to keep track of their flock. "Hevera, devera, and dick" corresponded to the numbers eight, nine, and ten. However, no one has yet offered to explain what a mouse and a clock have to do with sheepherding.

Like the words "tick tock," the curious phrase that begins this limerick could simply be an onomatoplasm—words that attempt to mimic a sound. "Hickory, dickory, dock" does convey the rhythm of a ticking clock. But these words are probably more akin to the counting-out phrase, "eenie, meenie, minie, moe."

In the early nineteenth century children used "Hickory, Dickory, Dock" as a count-out rhyme to decide who should begin a game or be chosen for a contest.

# London Bridge

London Bridge is broken down,
Broken down, broken down,
London Bridge is broken down,
My fair lady.

Build it up with wood and clay,
Wood and clay, wood and clay,
Build it up with wood and clay,
My fair lady.

Wood and clay will wash away,
wash away, wash away,
Wood and clay will wash away,
My fair lady.

Build it up with bricks and mortar,
Bricks and mortar, bricks and mortar,
Build it up with bricks and mortar,
My fair lady.

Bricks and mortar will not stay,
will not stay, will not stay,
Bricks and mortar will not stay,
My fair lady.

Build it up with iron and steel,
Iron and steel, iron and steel,
Build it up with iron and steel,
My fair lady.

Iron and steel will bend and bow,
Bend and bow, bend and bow,
Iron and steel will bend and bow,
My fair lady.

Build it up with silver and gold,
Silver and gold, silver and gold,
Build it up with silver and gold,
My fair lady.

Silver and gold will be stolen away,
Stolen away, stolen away,
Silver and gold will be stolen away,
My fair lady.

Set a man to watch all night,
Watch all night, watch all night,
Set a man to watch all night,
My fair lady.

The earliest text for London Bridge is also found in the 1744 publication TOMMY THUMB'S PRETTY SONG BOOK, but most experts believe the verse, and its accompanying game, is much older. Children in fourteenth-century Florence played a game in which two players formed a "bridge" with uplifted arms while others scurried under, trying to avoid being trapped when the arms came down around them.

But the song may have a darker side. Apparently early bridge construction required more than just sturdy materials and hard work. In an effort to appease the evil spirits lurking in the river, ancient bridge builders sometimes offered human sacrifices—they entombed people, especially children, in the foundations. These early engineers hoped the spirits of the buried ones would ward off supernatural forces, which for some reason were particularly intolerant of bridges. Curiously, there seemed to be no concern that these same spirits might instead seek revenge for being used as construction material.

# Old King Cole

Old King Cole
Was a merry old soul,
And a merry old soul was he;
He called for his pipe,
And he called for his bowl,
And he called for his fiddlers three.

Every fiddler, he had a fiddle,
And a very fine fiddle had he;
Twee tweedle dee, tweedle dee, went the fiddlers.
Oh, there's none so rare
As can compare
With King Cole and his fiddlers three.

The identity of this jovial king has been a matter of speculation for centuries. One theory claims that the song refers to the well-loved King Cole who ruled Britain in the third century. In the English town named Colchester, some ancient earthworks are still known locally as "King Cole's Kitchen."

Another explanation is that the merry old soul was a wealthy English clothier named Cole-brook, popularly known as Old Cole. Cole-brook allegedly had hundreds of servants. He may not have worn a crown, but he certainly lived like a king.

"Old King Cole" first appeared in print in 1708. The verse has subsequently appeared in several other forms, but no matter how the wording might vary, the rhyme retains the same theme—a carefree monarch with a fondness for tobacco and music.

# Hush-a-bye, Baby

Hush-a-bye, baby, on the tree top,
When the wind blows the cradle will rock;
When the bough breaks the cradle will fall,
Down will come baby, cradle, and all.

Cradles falling from treetops hardly seems a fitting subject for one of the most beloved lullabies in both England and America. Legend has it that a Pilgrim youth who sailed to America on the *Mayflower* composed "Hush-a-Bye, Baby" after watching a Native American mother hang her infant's birch-bark cradle on a tree branch. The wind supplied the power to rock the baby to sleep, and the gentle motion inspired the rhythm of the verse.

In the first printed version of "Hush-a-bye, Baby," found in a 1765 edition of MOTHER GOOSE'S MELODY, a footnote identified the rhyme as "a warning to the proud and ambitious who climb so high they generally fall at last." Modern readers, however, might offer a more practical interpretation: "before hanging your child's furniture from a tree, inspect the branch closely."

# Ring-a-Ring o' Roses

Ring-a-ring o' roses
A pocket full of posies,
A-tishoo! A-tishoo!
We all fall down.

For a time some scholars argued that this verse alluded to the Great Plague that swept through Europe in the fourteenth century. Supporters of the theory said that the ring of roses was actually the rash covering the victim's body, and the posies were the herbs and spices thought to ward off the sickness. The words "A-tishoo, A-tishoo" supposedly represented the sound of sneezing, one of the final symptoms before the unfortunate victims "fall down" in death.

Other experts disagree with this morbid explanation. They point out that the verse didn't appear in print until 1881—long after the Plague. Moreover, there are many different versions of the verse and game, most of which do not include the word "A-tishoo" and do not instruct the players to "fall down."

In any case, most children seem to agree that "Ring-a-ring o' roses"—a game in which you hold hands, walk round and round in a circle, and fall down at the end—is just plain fun.

# Tom, Tom, the Piper's Son

Tom, Tom, the piper's son,
Stole a pig and away he run;
The pig was eat
And Tom was beat,
And Tom went howling down the street.

A chapbook was
a small collection
of verse and
song.

A "pig" was a
pastry filled with
fruit.

Children are often uneasy or confused about the fate of this stolen pig. Modern illustrators have encouraged these concerns by incorrectly depicting Tom running away with a live pig. Rest easy. The animal in this rhyme is merely a pig-shaped pastry filled with fruit. These treats sold by street vendors were common in the eighteenth and nineteenth centuries.

The first written record of this rhyme appeared in an English chapbook during the late 1700s. Chapmen traveled the countryside peddling these popular little volumes of song and verse. In the early part of the nineteenth century, a number of books—all entitled TOM THE PIPER'S SON—celebrated the further adventures of Tom in rhyme and song.

# Jack and Jill

Jack and Jill went up the hill
    To fetch a pail of water;
Jack fell down and broke his crown,
    And Jill came tumbling after.

In the 1765 edition of MOTHER GOOSE'S MELODY, the characters fetching the pail of water were named Jack and Gill. The woodcut accompanying the rhyme depicted both children as boys. The artist apparently agreed with the interpreters who had theorized that the pair represented a well-known cardinal and bishop from the time of King Henry VIII.

But the Reverend Sabine Baring-Gould presented the theory that is now more widely accepted. In his 1866 book, CURIOUS MYTHS OF THE MIDDLE AGES, he claimed that Jack and Jill actually began as figures in a Scandinavian myth explaining the origin of the markings on the moon. It seems that Mani, the moon, captured two children, Hjuki and Bil, while they were filling a bucket with water. Ever since that fateful day, people who look at a full moon can, with a fair amount of imagination, make out the outline of the two with their bucket between them.

Through the years many verses have been added to the original six lines, but contemporary books usually carry only these two describing Jack's primitive first-aid treatment and Jill's harsh punishment for causing the catastrophe:

Up Jack got and home did trot,
    As fast as he could caper,
To old Dame Dob, who patched his nob
    With vinegar and brown paper.

When Jill came in, how she did grin,
    To see Jack's paper plaster;
Dame Dob, vexed, did whip her next
    For causing Jack's disaster.

# Humpty Dumpty

Humpty Dumpty sat on a wall,
Humpty Dumpty had a great fall.
All the king's horses,
And all the king's men,
Couldn't put Humpty together again.

Although today most people think of this verse as nothing more than the unlucky adventure of a hapless egg, "Humpty Dumpty" was originally a riddle. Readers were supposed to guess—without the aid of an illustration—that the answer was an egg. Experts think this riddle is thousands of years old.

Humpty is a popular figure around the globe. Kids in France know the unfortunate egg as *Boule, Boule*; Swedish youngsters call him *Thille Lille*. In Switzerland his name is *Annenadadeli*, and in parts of Germany it is *Rüntzelken-Püntzelken*.

**Humpty Dumpty was once the name of a popular drink.**

During the late seventeenth century, Humpty Dumpty was the name for a popular ale and brandy drink. The term "Humpty Dumpty" was also often used to describe a squat, comical person of either sex. In 1797, the rhyme called "Humpty Dumpty" appeared in print in Juvenile Amusements. Girls in nineteenth-century America played a game called Humpty Dumpty in which the players held their skirts tightly about their feet, rolled backwards, and tried to recover their balance without letting go of their skirts.

In 1872, Lewis Carroll immortalized Humpty Dumpty in the book Alice's Adventures Through the Looking Glass. "It's very provoking," Mr. Dumpty told Alice, "to be called an egg—very."

# Hey Diddle Diddle

Hey diddle diddle,
The cat and the fiddle,
The cow jumped over
    the moon;
The little dog laughed
To see such sport,
And the dish ran away
    with the spoon.

The six short lines of "Hey Diddle Diddle," one of the most popular nursery rhymes of all, have been the subject of much speculation and scholarly interpretation. Some theorize that the cat represents Queen Elizabeth and the little dog Robert Dudley, her favorite suitor. Others insist that the lines depict the antics of courtiers during the reign of Catherine of Aragon in the early 1500s. Still other scholars claim that the dish running away with the spoon symbolizes Richard III's seizure of the English throne.

It has also been speculated that the rhyme refers to the constellations of the night sky—Taurus (the bull) and Canis Minor (the little dog)—and that the moon-jumping might be connected to Hathor, the cow-headed Egyptian love goddess. One might be tempted to agree, however, with Sir Henry Reid. "I prefer to think," he said, "that it commemorates the athletic lunacy to which the strange conspiracy of the cat and the fiddle incited the cow."

# Rain, Rain, Go Away

Rain, rain, go away,
Come again another day.

Children have always made up songs or chants to ward off disappointments. Although "Rain, rain, go away" is the best-known example in English, it is only one of many similar verses. When dark clouds threatened, youngsters in ancient Greece would chant, "Come forth, come forth, beloved sun!" In seventeenth-century England, children tried to charm away wet weather by singing "Raine, raine, goe away, Come againe a Saterday." Other popular versions include "Rain, rain, go to Spain, Never show your face again" and "Rain, rain pour down, But not a drop on our town." It would be interesting to know if these charms were as popular with farmers' children...or if the lyrics changed during times of drought.

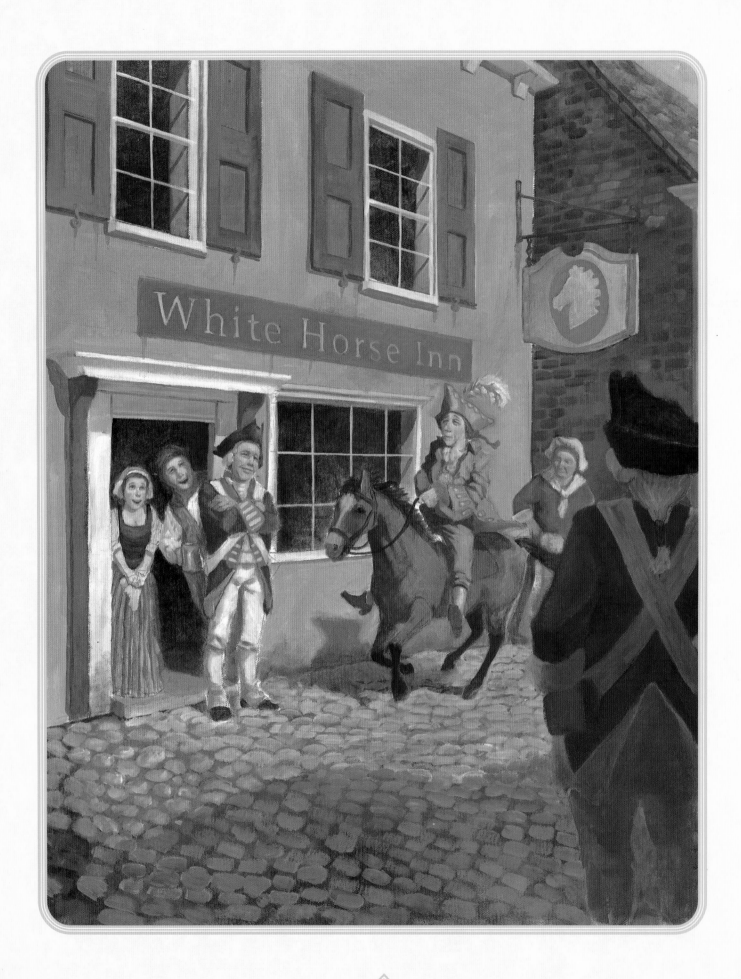

# Yankee Doodle Dandy

Yankee Doodle went to town,
Riding on a pony;
He stuck a feather in his cap,
And called it macaroni.

While no one knows exactly who composed this familiar melody, we can be reasonably certain that the words originated in America. At the outbreak of the American Revolution, British soldiers sang the well-known tune "Yankee Doodle Dandy" to ridicule the colonial troops. Americans adopted the popular ditty following their victory at the Battle of Bunker Hill, and it quickly became a song of defiance. In fact, it was reported that Washington's army marched toward Yorktown to the strains of "Yankee Doodle" just before General Cornwallis surrendered.

Why would Yankee Doodle refer to his feathered hat as a type of pasta? Actually he doesn't. Macaroni was a term used to describe a flamboyant, style-conscious individual, usually one who adopted the affected mannerisms of European nobility.

**A "macaroni"**

**was a foppish**

**young man.**

# 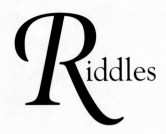iddles

Two legs sat upon three legs
With one leg in his lap;
In comes four legs
And runs away with one leg;
Up jumps two legs,
Catches up three legs,
Throws it after four legs,
And makes him bring back one leg.

In Spring I look gay,
Decked in comely array,
In Summer more clothing I wear;
When colder it grows,
I fling off my clothes,
And in Winter quite naked appear.

Black I am and much admired,
Men may seek me till they are tired;
I weary horse and comfort man,
Tell me this riddle if you can.

Two brothers we are,
    great burdens we bear,
By which we are bitterly pressed;
The truth is to say,
    we are full all the day,
And empty when we go to rest.

A shoemaker makes shoes without leather,
With all the four elements put together,
Fire, Water, Earth, Air,
And every customer takes two pair.

Hundreds of years ago, rhyming riddles were popular with adults as well as with children. These enjoyable little tests of wit were among the earliest literature printed exclusively for amusement. "Whiche was fyrst, ye henne or ye egge?" was included in WYNKYN DE WORDE'S AMUSING QUESTIONS, printed in 1511. The popularity of riddle-rhymes reached its peak during the Elizabethan Age, when many of them were extended and refined. Even Shakespeare alluded to them from time to time.

Today these puzzling verses live on in children's literature. Look closely at this illustration and you'll find the solutions to these once well-known riddles!

# _T_ongue Twisters

_T_ongue twisters, or tongue trippers, have been used for centuries as an aid in developing enunciation. PETER PIPER'S PRINCIPLES OF PLAIN AND PERFECT PRONUNCIATION, published in 1813, contained tongue twisters for every letter of the alphabet. Tongue-tripping lines are still widely used as enunciation exercises for actors—from students in the lowliest drama class to veterans in the prestigious Royal Academy of Dramatic Art. For almost as long, children have entertained themselves by seeing who can say tongue twisters the fastest.

Betty Botter bought some butter,
   But, she said, the butter's bitter;
If I put it in my batter
   It will make my batter bitter,
But a bit of better butter
   Will make my batter better.
So she bought a bit of butter
   Better than her bitter butter,
And she put it in her batter
   And the batter was not bitter.
So 'twas better Betty Botter
   bought a bit of better butter.

I need not your needles, they're needless to me;
For kneading of needles is needless, you see;
But did my neat trousers but need to be kneed,
I then should have need of your needles indeed.

How much wood would
   a woodchuck chuck
If a woodchuck could
   chuck wood?
He would chuck as much
   wood as a woodchuck
   could chuck
If a woodchuck could
   chuck wood.

Peter Piper picked a peck of pickled pepper;
A peck of pickled pepper Peter Piper picked;
If Peter Piper picked a peck of pickled pepper,
Where's the peck of pickled pepper Peter Piper picked?

The End